This book belongs to:

Ms Garbecki
10/05 ACSI conference

Tails from the Pantry
Little Life Lessons from Mom and Dad

Meatball

By Patsy Clairmont

Illustrated by Joni Oeltjenbruns

www.tommynelson.com

A Division of Thomas Nelson, Inc.
www.ThomasNelson.com

Published in Nashville, Tennessee, by Tommy Nelson®, a Division of Thomas Nelson, Inc.

Tommy Nelson books may be purchased in bulk for educational, business, fundraising, or sales promotional use. For information, please email SpecialMarkets@ThomasNelson.com

ISBN: 1-4003-0561-6

Printed in the United States of America
05 06 07 08 PHX 5 4 3 2 1

This little series is dedicated to Justin and Noah. . . .

How blessed I am to have two "little mouse" grandsons who regularly nibble in my pantry. Darlings, leave all the crumbs you want in Nana's house. I'll tidy up later. Always heed Mommy and Daddy's lessons about staying safe. You are both loved "a bushel and a peck and a hug around the neck."

~Nana

APPLE
JUICE

Once upon a can of spaghetti sat a mouse named Meatball MacKenzie. Yes, Meatball. Her daddy, Mac, named her after his favorite snack.

"It could have been worse," her mother, Lily, admitted. "He almost named you after his favorite cheese—Limburger."

Lily, thinking her daughter's name was not very girly, painted Meatball's toenails powder puff pink and painted polka dots on her daughter's naturally curly tail.

Meatball liked to practice climbing, which was why she was perched atop the spaghetti can on a shelf in the pantry.

As she was looking around the kitchen, she spotted Duff, the Calico cat. Duff seemed to be the size of an 18-wheeler to Meatball. So when he dropped down on his haunches and began inching across the floor in her direction, Meatball knew she was in trouble.

Meatball jumped from the spaghetti can down onto a can of tuna fish and from there, slid down onto a jar of pears. Without pausing, she darted behind a chubby bag of flour.

Just then Duff, who was now inside the pantry, swatted his furry paw at Meatball's polka dotted tail. But instead of hitting Meatball, Duff smacked the side of the flour bag, causing a great white cloud.

SPAGHETTI
DRIED
MPKIN

When the air cleared, Duff had flour in his eyes and up his freckled nose. Duff sneezed . . .

ah-choo,

ah-ah-choo,

ah-ah-ah-choo . . .

three times.

That last sneeze was a doozy, throwing Duff backward out of the pantry.

Meatball was coated in flour from her nose to her toes. She spotted an open box of cornflakes on the shelf below her, and when Duff sneezed for the third time, Meatball jumped into the cereal box. Then she burrowed deep into the flakes and lay very still.

Meatball's heart was thumping wildly with fear, but she didn't let out a squeak.

Meatball remembered her mother's safety rules against all cats, misguided bats, and bully rats:

1. **Scurry to safety.**
2. **Be still.**
3. **Wait patiently.**

Meatball waited and waited and waited. In fact, she waited so long she fell fast asleep. When she woke up, all was quiet. Certain Duff was curled up somewhere napping, Meatball decided it was time to venture out of the cereal box.

Meatball wanted to scamper home, which was three shelves up where she lived in a forgotten box of Christmas candy with her family. Her bedroom was right next to a chocolate-covered cherry that she'd been nibbling on for months. Oh, how yummy that sounded right now to her growling tummy!

Meatball crawled on top of the cornflakes and looked up, up, up, to the top of the box. "Oh dear, how am I going to get out of here?" she said out loud.

Meatball tried jumping, but she couldn't jump high enough. And the harder she tried, the more afraid she became. Then she remembered her dad's words: ***"Think before you jump."*** So, Meatball sat down on the cornflakes to think.

Meatball decided to wiggle around to see if there was another way out. She was about to give up when she bumped into something that wasn't a cornflake. It wasn't food of any kind, and it wasn't cardboard like the box. It was something hard, and it made a crinkly sound when she stepped on it.

"Hmmm . . ." Meatball carefully nibbled at the plastic wrap until she could see what was inside. It was a prize—a whistle!

Meatball dragged the whistle to the top of the flakes and then gave it a toot, hoping her family would hear and come to her rescue. She was certain they must be out looking for her.

Tweet, Tweet, Tweet.

She blew on the whistle again and again.

Tweet, Tweet, Tweet.

Then she heard someone call her name.

"Meatball! Meatball!" It was her dad.

"Here, Daddy, here! Inside the cornflakes!"

Peering down into the box, her daddy shouted, "Oh, my little Meatball! You're safe!" Never had her name sounded so wonderful to her little ears.

"We'll get you out," he promised, "but you must do as I say. Dig your way into the center of the cereal and roll up into a ball. Your mom, brother, and I will tip the box over so you can climb out."

"But, Daddy, I'm scared."

"Yes, I know. Being scared is okay, Meatball. Feeling afraid doesn't have to keep you from being brave. So hurry now."

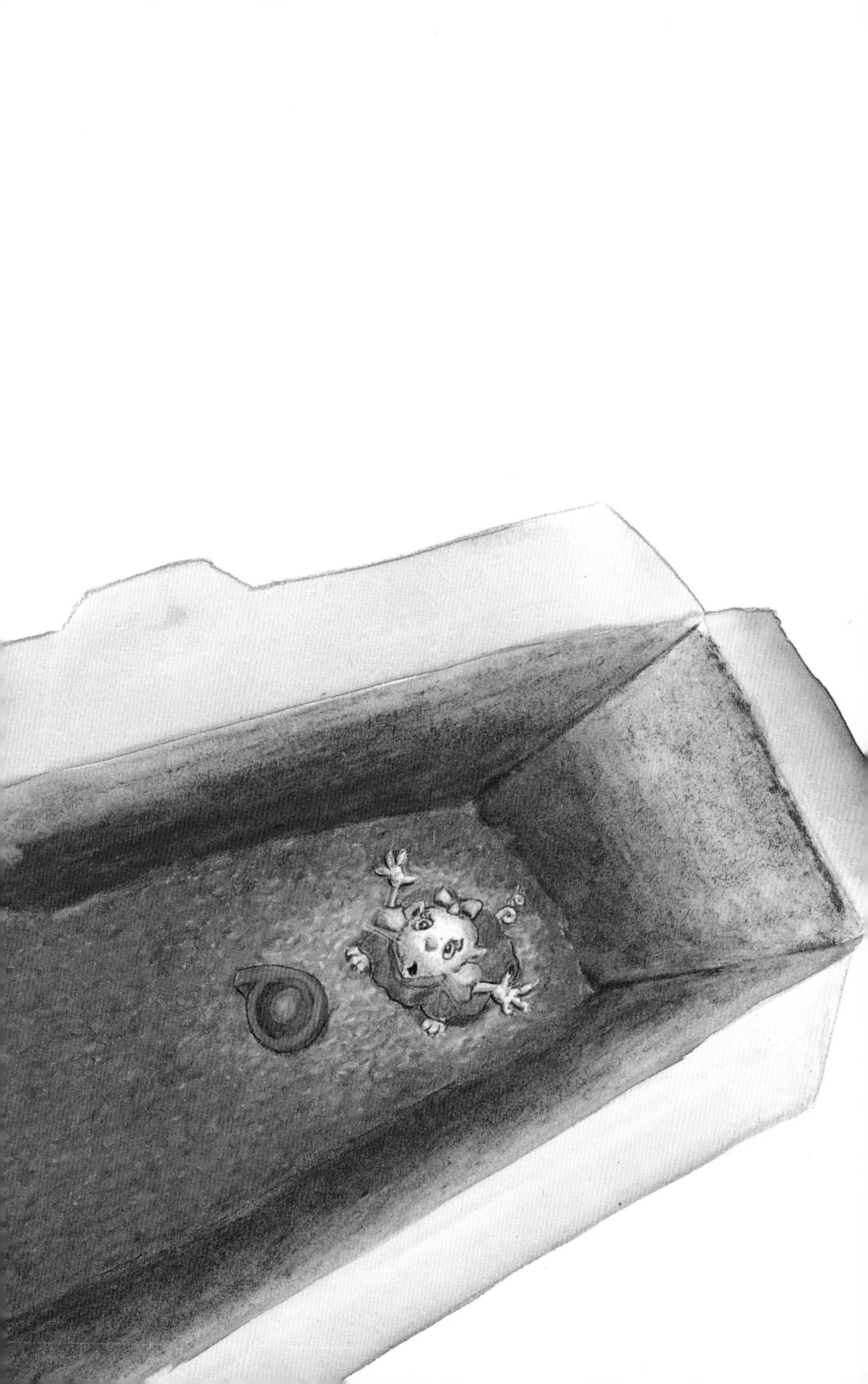

Meatball dug her way into the flakes and tucked herself into a furry ball. Within moments, she felt the box tipping back and forth, back and forth. And down it went onto the shelf. Meatball could feel herself tumbling, and the next thing she knew, she rolled right out of the box!

"Hooray!" they all cheered.

Meatball and her family had a happy reunion, and to celebrate, they feasted on—what else?—spaghetti! What better way is there to celebrate a Meatball?